Storytime Id[eas for]
CIRCLE TIME

Tips and techniques for successful storytelling

By JEAN WARREN • Illustrated by PRISCILLA BURRIS

Totline₀ Publications
A Division of Frank Schaffer Publications, Inc.
Torrance, California

Totline Publications would like to thank the following people for their contributions to this book: Sue Brown, Louisville, KY; Patty Claycomb, Ventura, CA; Cindy Dingwall, Palatine, IL; Sue Foster, Mukilteo, WA; Angela Metzendorf, Kinsman, OH.

Editor: Kathleen Cubley
Contributing Editors: Carol Gnojewski, Susan Hodges, Elizabeth McKinnon, Susan M. Sexton
Copyeditor: Kris Fulsaas
Proofreader: Miriam Bulmer
Editorial Assistant: Durby Peterson
Graphic Designer (Interior): Sarah Ness
Layout Artist: Gordon Frazier
Graphic Designer (Cover): Brenda Mann Harrison
Illustrator (Cover): Barb Tourtillotte
Production Manager: Melody Olney

ISBN: 1-57029-241-8

Library of Congress Catalog Card Number 98-61459
Printed in the United States of America
Published by Totline® Publications

Business Office: 23740 Hawthorne Blvd.
Torrance, CA 90505

Introduction

Storytime Ideas for Circle Time is designed as a reference book for preschool teachers, offering quick, easy tips and ideas to make storytime successful and fun, and to integrate learning, too.

There are four types of storytelling that are all appropriate for preschoolers. Using a variety of the following storytelling methods will keep children interested and involved.

+ Tell a story exactly as an author has written it, stopping to show the pictures as you go along.

+ Tell a story in your own words while showing the pictures from a book.

+ Tell a story using props, such as puppets or flannelboard figures.

+ Tell stories by dramatizing the actions with hand motions and body movement.

Stories are great for helping children calm down after high-energy activities and for helping children learn to focus their attention. Through stories, children can also learn about feelings, about other people, about their environment, and about the world beyond their neighborhood. Stories can introduce children to humor, real happenings, and make-believe. Stories can strengthen memory and imagination skills. You can also use storytime to teach lessons through nonthreatening scenarios.

Perhaps the most important learning opportunity storytime provides is the introduction of language skills. By repeating colorful phrases in stories, children will learn that words are used for meaning and for fun. Through repetitious stories, children learn to make predictions. When children retell a story, they learn beginning sequencing. Children who have listened to and repeated stories are well on their way to learning about the structure of stories (beginning, middle, ending) and about recognizing familiar plots and similarities and differences in things.

There is really no right or wrong group size for storytime. It all depends on your children, the help you have, and what you are comfortable with. Some experts recommend small group sizes, which is probably ideal, but my theory—no matter how many children you have in your group—is that the more you keep your children involved, the more they will pay attention and the more they will gain from the experience. When children sit and listen to a story, they are using one sense—hearing. Because preschool children learn through all their senses, the more senses you involve, the better.

I hope that you find this collection of storytime ideas helpful and that it enables you to turn your storytime into a shared experience of fun, relaxed time.

Jean Warren

Contents

Attention-Getting Ideas

Storytime Train

Gathering young children together in a group and then getting and keeping their attention is sometimes the most challenging part of storytime. Songs and rhymes are a wonderfully fun and easy way to call your children together and get them excited about storytime. "Storytime Train" is a great technique for beginning your storytelling session.

When you are all set up for storytime, start roaming around the room repeating the rhyme "Storytime Train." Your children will know when they see and hear you chugging around the room to put away their current activity and join the train by holding on to your back. As soon as most of the children are part of the train, lead them into the storytime area. Have the children sit down in their usual storytime seating arrangement.

Storytime Train

Story train, story train
Chugging down the track.
If you want a story,
Hook on to my back.

Story train, story train
Chugging all around.
When everyone's aboard,
We'll all sit down.

Jean Warren

Story Chime

Prepare for this activity by having a bell on hand at the storytelling area. Tell your children that the bell is the story chime and that you will ring the chime when everyone is ready. Find one or two children who are ready for storytime. Bring them with you into the storytelling area and sing the song "I'm So Happy" (below) to them. Have them do the motions and then sit down. When other children hear their friends singing the song, they will put their things away and join you in the story area. Have the seated children sing with you as the new group of children does the motions and then sits down. Repeat until all the children are seated. Then, ring the story chime and begin the story.

I'm So Happy

Sung to: "If You're Happy and You Know It"

I'm so happy that you've come to storytime,
So listen very carefully to my rhyme.
Stand up straight and stomp your feet.
Clap twice, then take your seat.
We'll begin when I ring the story chime.

Jean Warren

Would You Like to Hear a Story?

To announce that storytime is about to begin, walk around the room singing the song "Would You Like to Hear a Story?" Join hands with your children as they follow you to the storytime area. Walk in a circle as you repeat the song together. Sit down as a group when all of the children have joined the circle.

Would You Like to Hear a Story?
Sung to: "Mary Had a Little Lamb"

Would you like to hear a story,
Hear a story, hear a story?
Would you like to hear a story?
Then come with me.

Angela Metzendorf

More Attention-Getting Songs

Time for Stories

Sung to: "Clementine"

Time for stories, time for stories,

Time for stories today.

Let's be quiet, pay attention,

Wonder what we'll hear today?

Cindy Dingwall

If You're Ready

Sung to: "If You're Happy and You Know It"

If you're ready for a story, find a seat.

If you're ready for a story, find a seat.

Check your hands and then your feet.

If you're ready, find a seat.

If you're ready for a story, find a seat.

Sue Brown

This song encourages your children to find a spot to sit down in front of you. It gently reminds them to quiet their hands and their feet so that storytime can begin.

Quick Attention Grabbers

Subtle actions sometimes work the best to signal to your children that it's time for a story. Try some of the following fun and easy ideas for gathering busy children together and getting (and then keeping) their attention during storytime.

Lower Your Voice—Instead of raising your voice to get your children's attention, try lowering your voice. As children strain to hear what you are saying, they will lower their own noise level.

Flash the Lights—This usually gets immediate results, especially if you have used it with your children previously to tell them to stop what they are doing and to listen for your announcement.

Story Mats—Many teachers like using story mats for storytime. Carpet squares, small towels, or placemats make great story mats. The nice thing about story mats is that they provide a clearly defined space for each child. When your children see you setting out the story mats, it is a visual reminder that they should put away what they are doing and come to storytime.

Story Chime—Look for a special bell that you can bring into your classroom and use to capture your children's attention. A large jingle bell or a cowbell works well.

Marble Jar—Place several marbles in a glass jar. When you shake the jar, your children will look up to see what is going on. When you have their attention, let them know it is storytime.

Story Drum—Bring a small drum into the story area. Sit down and start beating the drum with your hand. When a child joins you, give him or her the drum to beat. Pass the drum to other children as they join the group. When everyone arrives and has had a turn beating the drum, your storytime can begin.

Attention-Grabbing Props

Story Hat—Make a simple hat and use it to announce storytime. First, attach Velcro to a hat. Then add some felt story characters to the front of the hat and walk around the room. Your children will be curious about the story characters and eager to get to storytime to find out more about them.

Story Chair—Often teachers have a special chair that they designate as the "story chair." When your children see you sitting in this chair, they know they should gather around to hear a story.

Story Flag—Put up a small flag holder in your story area. When it is storytime, put up a flag you designate as the "story flag." Your story flag can be a decorative purchased one (for instance, from a garden store) or one you create yourself out of felt or colorful fabric.

Keeping Kids' Attention

Getting children gathered for storytime is sometimes just half the battle. Now that you have them seated, how do you keep their attention until everyone is ready? Here are some unique ideas to keep everyone occupied, interested, and having fun.

Books—Pass books out to your children as they enter the story area. Have them look quietly at the books while they are waiting for the other children to get ready. Collect the books before storytime begins.

Fingerplays—One surefire way to capture children's attention is to focus the action on yourself. By doing simple fingerplays, children enjoy waiting for others to get ready. Try one or both of the following favorites.

The Eensy Weensy Spider

The eensy weensy spider

Crawled up the water spout.
  (Crawl fingers up high.)

Down came the rain and

Washed the spider out.
  (Drop fingers quickly.)

Out came the sun and

Dried up all the rain,
  (Form circle with arms.)

And the eensy weensy spider

Crawled up the spout again.
  (Crawl fingers back up high.)

Traditional

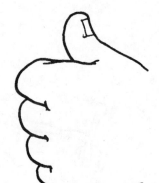

Where Is Thumbkin?

Where is Thumbkin?

Where is Thumbkin?
  (Put hands behind back.)

Here I am!
  (Bring one thumb forward.)

Here I am!
  (Bring other thumb forward.)

How are you today, sir?
  (Wiggle one thumb.)

Very well, I thank you.
  (Wiggle other thumb.)

Run away. Run away.
  (Put hands behind back.)

Traditional

Wiggle Worms

If your children seem really restless before starting your storytime, give them some Wiggle Worms!

To prepare for this strategy, cut brown yarn into 6-inch lengths to make "wiggle worms," and place them in a box.

As your children gather for circle time, recite the first verse of the "Wiggle Worm Rhyme" at right. Hold out the box of wiggle worms for them to look at. Continue reciting the rhyme, having the children do the actions as described in the rhyme.

Wiggle Worm Rhyme

Here are some worms who are, oh, so sad.

They've lost all the wiggles that they once had.

They wonder if you, just for today,

Would lend them your wiggles so they can play.
(Let each child select a wiggle worm from the box.)

Wiggle them up and wiggle them down.
(Shake wiggle worms up and down.)

Wiggle your worms around and around.
(Move wiggle worms in a circle.)

Wiggle them high and wiggle them low.
(Shake wiggle worms over head and near floor.)

Wiggle them fast and wiggle them slow.
(Shake wiggle worms quickly, then slowly.)

Wiggle them over your shoes and your socks.
(Shake wiggle worms over feet.)

Then wiggle them back up to their box.
(Drop wiggle worms in box.)

Thank you for sharing your wiggles today.

You'll get them all back when it's your time to play.

Now that your wiggles are all gone from you,

I'll tell you just what we are going to do.

Patty Claycomb

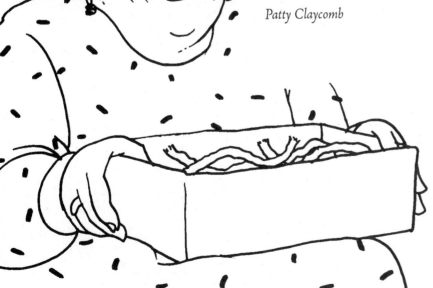

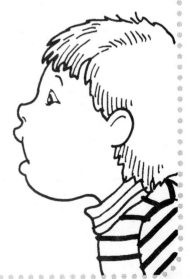

Special Friend

Another activity to ensure your group's quiet participation is to bring along a special friend. A special friend is a special stuffed animal that is very shy and will only stay in the group if your children are quiet. Before beginning the activity, hide the special friend in the storytelling area.

Special Friend

Let's get together
And all sit down.
If we're quiet
And don't make a sound,
A special friend
Will come today.
I sure do hope
She'll want to stay.

Take the special friend out of her hiding place and set it where all the children can see it. Explain that the animal is very shy and will run back to its hiding place if it gets scared. If the children become restless and noisy, pick up the animal and act as if it is going to run away as you say the following rhyme:

Oh, little friend, don't run away.
We'll be quiet if you stay.
Please come and sit with us once more.
We'll be quiet, like before!

Patty Claycomb

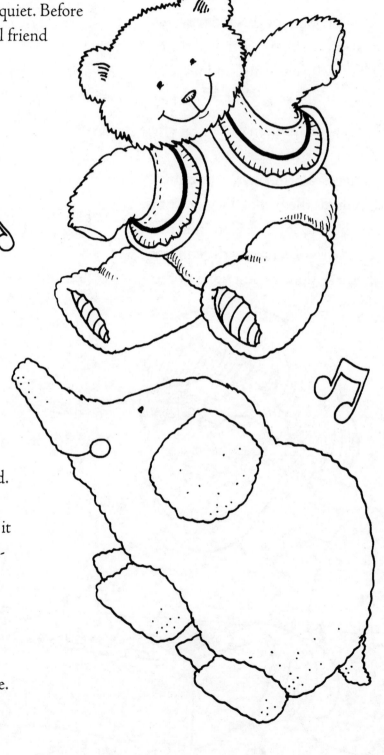

I See a Bird

This a great quieting activity your children will love. Begin by quietly saying, "Repeat after me. Repeat after me." Repeat until all of the children are focused on you. Explain that you are going to recite a rhyme together. First you will say a line and then the children will repeat it exactly. Begin reciting "I See a Bird," adding the motions as indicated.

I See a Bird

Teacher: I see a bird
(Place hand above eyes and peer around.)

Children: I see a bird

Teacher: Up in a tree.
(Point up.)

Children: Up in a tree.

Teacher: If I sit very still
(Sit still.)

Children: If I sit very still

Teacher: It will fly to me!
(Make flapping motion with one hand.)

Children: It will fly to me!

Teacher: Now if I'm as quiet
(Hold finger to lips.)

Children: Now if I'm as quiet

Teacher: As I can be,

Children: As I can be,

Teacher: It'll sit on my shoulder
(Place hand on shoulder.)

Children: It'll sit on my shoulder

Teacher: And watch with me.

Children: And watch with me.

Patty Claycomb

Tell the children that if they move too much, their "birds" might fly away. Then continue with your planned storytime activity. At the end of the story, let the children fly away with their birds.

Story Show-and-Tell

Children enjoy stories much more when the objects in the story have meaning to them. If the story is about a pumpkin, for example, and you suspect that some of your children have never experienced a real pumpkin, bring one in. Let your children examine it and discover its characteristics before you begin your story.

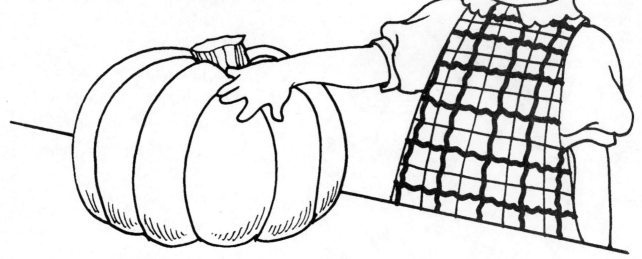

Previous Experiences

Previous experiences give special meaning to stories. If you have the opportunity to go on any field trips with your children, try to find related stories to share with them afterward. Experiences can also come from things that happen around your center. Some events that might trigger special storytelling sessions include working outside, bulldozers or other tractor-type vehicles driving down the street, a firefighter visit, or another visitor from the community.

Be sure to share your past experiences with your children when telling a story. If the story is about snow and you had fun as a child making a snowman, tell your children about your experience. Bring in photographs if you have them.

Story Chest

Children love surprises. You might bring in a small chest, a large bag, or an interesting container. For several days, place a special story treat in the story chest. It could be an object or a snack related to the story, or even a letter from the main character of the story. Keeping the surprise hidden until just before you read or tell the story adds suspense and anticipation. Your children will soon look forward to the surprise and to storytime each day.

Story Line

A clothesline is a wonderful tool to use during storytime. Try hanging photocopied pictures of story characters from the "story line." Let your children hang the characters in the order of their appearance in the story, or let them mix them up and tell their own version of the story.

Variation: Instead of a story line, make a story mobile. Use string to hang pictures of characters from the bottom wire of a coat hanger. Then hang the mobile representing the day's story in the story area.

Giant Story Characters

For a fun surprise, photocopy and then enlarge the main character in the story of the day. Try to photocopy the character as lightly as possible so that you can color it with bright-colored felt tip markers. Place the giant character in a prominent place in your room and let your children guess who their special visitor is.

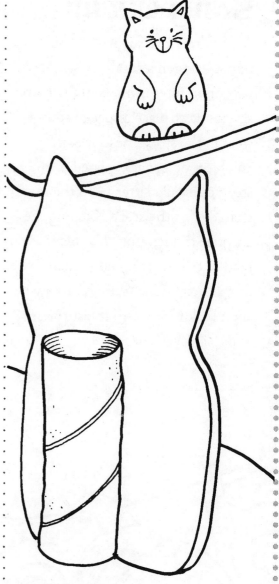

Standup Characters

Make standup characters by photocopying story characters, coloring them, cutting them out, and then taping them to a toilet tissue tube. Place them in the block area or home-life center for your children to play with before and after your storytime.

General Storytelling Tips

Be Prepared

Be sure that you have all of your materials on hand before you begin storytime. When you are trying to keep young children's attention, one sure way to quickly lose it is to have to run and get something, or to have some important object missing.

Avoid Interruptions

Let your fellow teachers know when you plan to have storytime and ask that they not disturb your class during this time. A sign on your door may save you a distracted class.

Keep Kids Focused

Children have an easier time staying focused if they are somehow involved in the story. Instead of asking your children to sit around you while you tell the story, keep children active and involved.

Use Voice Inflection

When speaking or reading to your children, vary volume and voice characterizations, emphasize important words, and imitate story sounds with your voice. For example, make the teeny-tiny mouse speak in a teeny-tiny voice and make the lion's voice loud and roaring.

Use Sound Effects

If at all possible, use real sound effects when telling a story. Nothing gets and keeps children's attention more than the use of real sounds. Bring in a bell to ring, a rainmaker to let your children hear the rain, or animal toys that make animal sounds. Even your own hands and feet can provide attention-getting sound effects.

Puppets, Flannelboard, & Magnetboard Ideas

Story Mitts

Story mitts are especially popular with young children. You can purchase a story mitt or make one with little effort. Almost any kind of glove will work, but gardening gloves are inexpensive and work well for this purpose. Glue Velcro fasteners (found in fabric stores) onto the tips of one or both gloves. Create story characters out of felt scraps or pompoms and glue Velcro circles onto their backs. As you introduce each character in your story, attach it to a Velcro-tipped finger.

Since story mitts are usually too large for children to use, let them join in the fun by holding the characters while you read the story and attaching them to the mitt at the appropriate time in the story.

Stick Puppets

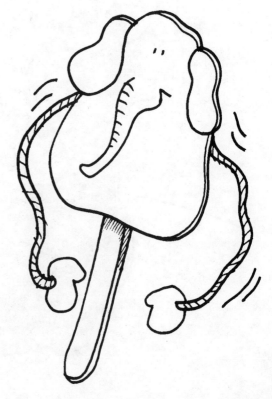

Stick puppets are some of the easiest types of puppets to make. Decorate cardboard shapes with fabric scraps, pompoms, and felt tip markers and then attach craft sticks or straws to the back of the shapes. For additional action from the puppets, add yarn arms. Cut yarn approximately 4 inches long and glue or tape small hand mitts to each end. Then tape the middle of the yarn to the back of the puppet. When you twist the stick, the arms will move.

Variation: Make quick and easy stick puppets by cutting characters from old birthday cards.

Paper Finger Puppets

Finger puppets can be made from heavy paper. Simply cut out puppet shapes as shown in the illustration. Cut slits into the top of one end of the rectangular strip and at the bottom of the other end, as shown, so the ends can be joined around the finger. Decorate the puppets with felt tip markers, felt pieces, pompoms, or googly eyes.

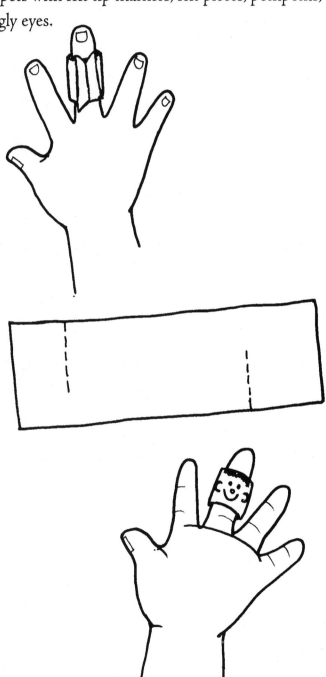

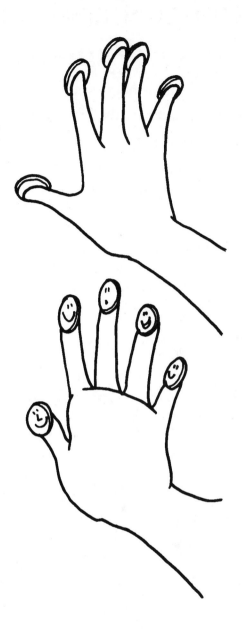

Sticker Finger Puppets

To make these super-simple puppets, draw faces on plain round stickers. Attach them to the ends of your fingers and you have instant finger puppets. Children love to make and wear these puppets.

Rolled-Paper Finger Puppets

Make simple finger puppets by rolling and taping the ends of a 2-inch-wide strip of paper together and sliding it onto your finger. Decorate the puppets to go with your story of the day.

Variation: To make a spider puppet, fringe the bottom of the paper to make eight legs.

Folded-Paper Finger Puppets

Cut a 5-by-5-inch rectangle out of construction paper. Fold the rectangle in half lengthwise and then in half again to make a long, narrow strip. Curl one of the ends down and fasten it in place with a paper clip, as shown in the illustration. Add a face with a felt tip marker and tie yarn around the top of the curled paper to make hair. To use the puppet, insert your finger in the folds at the bottom of the puppet.

Walking Puppets

Children are always fascinated with walking puppets. Cut a torso and head shape from cardboard. Cut two finger-size holes at the bottom. Insert your middle and index fingers into the holes and move your fingers to make the puppet walk.

Hint: A quick way to cut the finger holes is to fold the bottom of the shape upward and cut half circles on the fold.

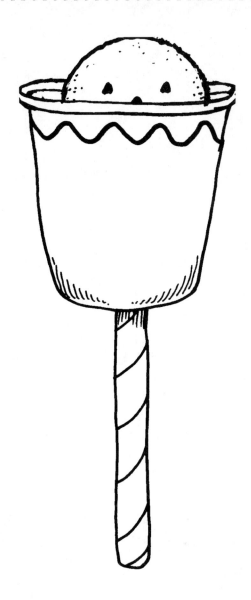

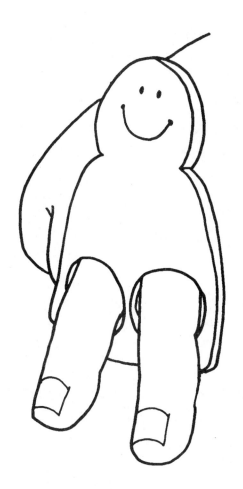

Pop-Up Puppets

A pop-up puppet is sure to delight your children and get their attention. Insert one end of a straw about $1/2$ inch into a $1\,1/2$-inch diameter plastic-foam ball and then pull the straw out. Drop some glue into the hole and insert the straw again. After allowing the glue to dry, use felt tip markers to draw on eyes, a nose, and a mouth. Poke a hole in the bottom of a paper cup. Insert the straw in the hole while holding the cup upright. Use the straw to pop the puppet up out of the cup or to hide it inside the cup.

Hand Puppets

Most hand puppets are made from felt squares. Since they require some sewing, this is a great project to turn over to parent volunteers. Try to make some puppets large, to fit your hand, and some small, to fit your children's hands. To make a puppet, cut two body shapes (as shown in the illustration) out of felt. Stack them together and stitch approximately ¼ inch from the edge, leaving the bottom edge open. Glue on pieces of felt to make faces and clothes. If you want puppets with ears, insert the ear shapes between the shapes before sewing them together.

Tip: For a less durable but quick and inexpensive hand puppet, cut body shapes out of heavy paper towels and tape them together.

Paper-Sack Puppets

Paper sacks make easy and inexpensive talking puppets. To make one, place a small paper bag flat on a table with the flap at the top. Make the flap into a face by drawing on facial features with a felt tip marker. Add hats, hair, or clothing by gluing on construction paper shapes as desired.

Brush Puppets

Almost any brush can be converted into a puppet. Glue googly eyes and a yarn mouth on the back of the brush to make a puppet. Using the same method, even fly swatters or pancake turners can be made into puppets.

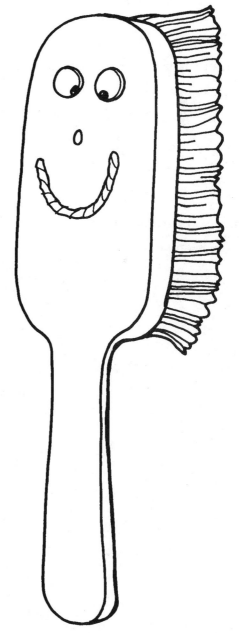

Paper-Cup Puppets

Paper cups make quick and easy puppets. In the side of a paper cup, make a hole large enough for your finger. Glue a construction paper nose to the bottom of the cup and eyes to the side of the cup opposite the finger hole. Add other facial features as desired. Drape a white napkin over your finger before sticking it in the cup, to make a quick robe that covers your hand.

Paper Plate Puppet Stage

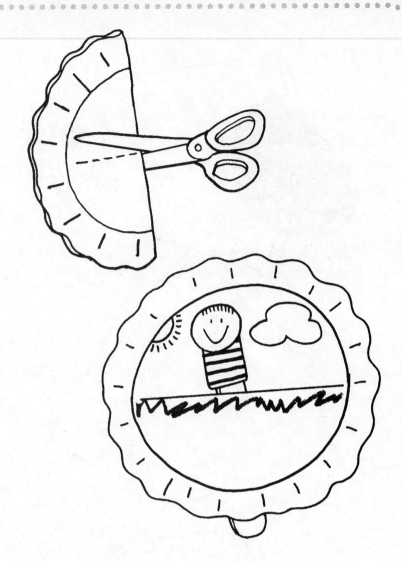

Although you do not need a stage for most puppets, a few finger puppets require some background. To make a quick stage, fold a paper plate in half and cut a slit in the center of the fold, leaving at least 1 inch on each edge. When you open the plate, you'll have a slit across the center. Decorate the top half of the plate as the background and the bottom half of the plate as the foreground. Place your finger or a stick puppet in the slit to stage an appealing puppet show.

Hint: To avoid paper cuts, place tape over each edge of the slit after decorating the plate.

Tissue Box Stage

Another simple puppet stage can be made from a tissue box. Cut a large hole in the bottom of the box. Insert a variety of puppets through the hole to perform on the stage.

Tree-House Stage

Toilet tissue tubes make unique tree-house stages for squirrels and birds. Cut a hole in the side of the tube and then tape real or paper branches to the top. To use the stage, insert a finger puppet through the bottom of the tube and have it peek out through the hole in the side of the tube.

Variation: To make a larger tree-house stage, cut the bottom off an oatmeal container and glue brown construction paper around the outside of the container. Add branches to the top and a hole in the side to complete the stage.

Box Stage

Lay a cardboard box on its side. Cut a rectangle out of the top half of the box bottom. Add background decorations to the box, if desired. Place your hand puppets in through the back of the box to stage your puppet show.

Gameboard Flannelboards

When game pieces are lost, don't throw away the gameboards—cover them with felt to make great flannelboards. Lay the board on top of a piece of felt. Cut around the board, leaving a 2- to 3-inch edge of felt. Fold the edges over onto the back of the board and secure with tape. You can even fold your new flannelboard in the middle for easy storage.

Carpet Flannelboards

Small pieces of flat indoor-outdoor carpeting can be used as a substitute for a flannelboard. Use small carpet squares to make individual boards for your children.

Apron Flannelboards

Children love flannelboard activities even more when you *are* the flannelboard! You can make a simple story apron out of an inexpensive butcher's apron (available at most kitchen or import stores, or look for them at thrift stores). Most aprons come with two large pockets at the bottom. Sew two light blue felt squares onto the apron above the pockets. Sew two green felt squares to the front of the pockets. Now you have a grass and sky background for your flannelboard story.

Variation: To make an indoor background, simply sew on beige-colored felt squares.

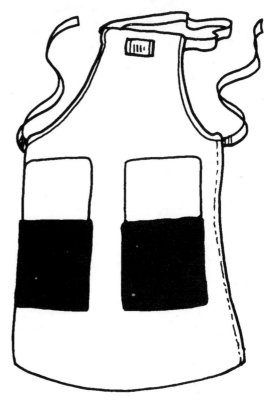

Room Divider Flannelboards

Bookcases and other room dividers make great flannelboards. Position a divider for easy access during storytime. Cover the back with felt or flannel. The edges can be tacked, stapled, or taped into place. Now you not only have a handy flannelboard, but you've also brightened up the back of what is often a boring piece of furniture.

Coloring Book Characters

Beginning coloring books are the best places to find simple patterns for flannelboard shapes. Simply cut out the image, pin it to a piece of felt, and cut the shape out of felt. Then add features with permanent markers or felt pieces.

If you want more-detailed characters, color the image with felt tip markers, cut out the shape, and glue it onto a piece of felt. After trimming the felt around the image, you will have a story character ready to cling to your flannelboard.

Pattern Book Characters

Craft stores and school supply stores often carry pattern books that are perfect for making all kinds of storybook characters. Rather than cutting up your pattern books, make copies of the patterns that you want to use. Use the same methods described for the Coloring Book Characters to make Pattern Book Characters. Patterns with simple, recognizable characters in outline form work best.

Using Magazine Pictures

Old magazines and catalogs seem to be the standby for just about everything we teach or do in preschool. You may already have a handy file of pictures you've collected, but if you don't, start today and save magazine pictures of children, animals, seasons, food, or any other preschool topic.

To use the pictures on your flannelboard, first glue them onto an index card or thin cardboard. Trim around the edges, then glue felt strips on the back, or try some of the backing ideas listed on pages 38 and 39.

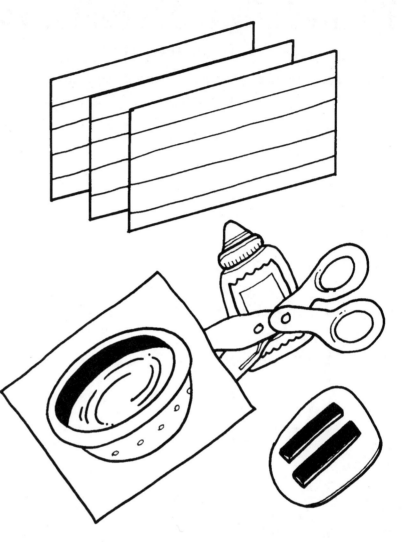

Using Old Books

Thrift stores and garage sales are wonderful places to find inexpensive, used children's books. Even if the edges of the book are a little worn, the pictures can be used on your flannelboard. Cut them out and back them as you would magazine pictures.

If you are lucky enough to find two identical books, you will have access to all the pictures and you do not have to choose which side of the page to cut up.

Flannelboard Character Backing Ideas

You don't need to spend a lot of money backing your flannelboard characters. There are common products that work well as flannelboard character backing. Here are some ideas to try.

Spray Glue—Spray the backs of flannelboard characters with spray glue. Characters made from paper stick well with this method. If glue stops adhering, simply spray the characters again. (Be sure to use spray adhesives well away from your children.)

Velcro Circles—Self-stick Velcro circles are great for attaching characters made out of paper, light wood, or any other material that would not ordinarily adhere to flannel.

Felt Strips—Glue paper characters to sturdy, lightweight cardboard. Trim around the edges, then glue on felt strips so the characters will adhere to the flannel.

Sandpaper Strips—Cut sandpaper into strips and glue a strip to the back of your flannelboard characters.

Tape—In an emergency, rolled tape will hold characters in place. The holding power only lasts for a short time because the fibers from the flannel soon cover most of the sticky part of the tape.

Sponge-Type Dryer Sheets—If you use sponge-type fabric softeners in your dryer, save them after use for great flannelboard character backers.

Paper Towel Cutouts—When you use paper towels to make your flannelboard characters, you don't need a backing. The towels are textured enough to cling on their own to the flannelboard. These characters are great for one-time use.

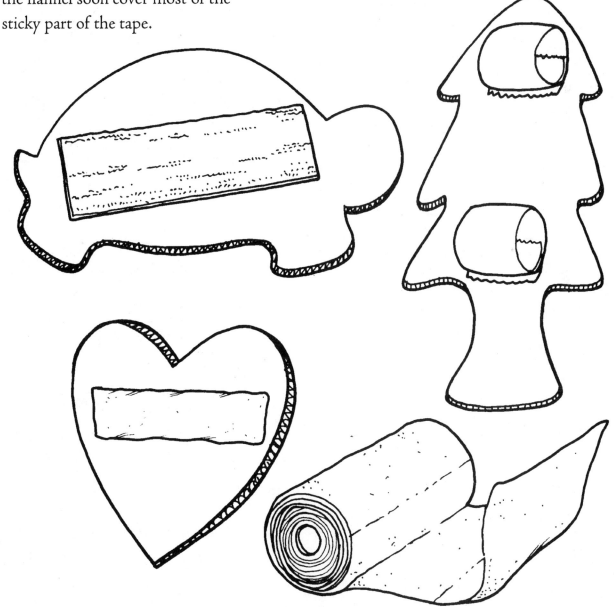

Baking-Sheet Magnetboards

Non-aluminum baking sheets make great magnet-boards. You can jazz them up easily by adding a self-stick paper background. Cover the top half of the cookie sheet with light blue self-stick paper and the bottom half with green self-stick paper. Other features may also be added if you are working with a particular theme.

Burner Covers

For a smaller but very handy magnetboard, you can use metal burner covers that are sold to fit over stove burners. These can also be covered with self-stick paper, if desired. Children will love working with these small, personal magnetboards.

Screen Magnetboard

To make this fun magnetboard, simply sandwich a square of metal screening between a piece of light-weight fabric and a piece of corrugated cardboard. Use duct tape to secure all of the edges.

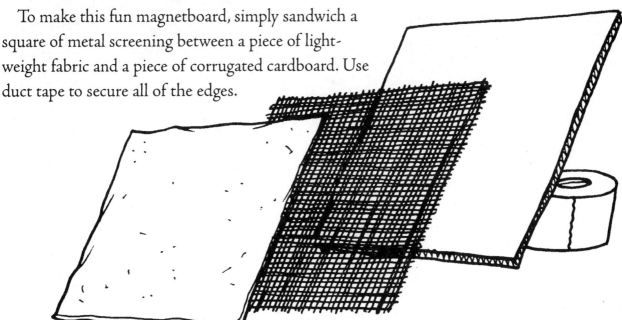

Refrigerator-Door Magnetboard

If you have a refrigerator in your center, let your children use it for magnet fun. You may also be able to find an old refrigerator door at a junkyard. Hang the door on a wall in your center. The children will love telling stories with magnets on the door.

Pancake Turners

This idea is a real hit with young children. Bring in two to five pancake turners. Let your children hold them up while you attach a story character to each one. Have the children hold up the appropriate character when it is mentioned in the story.

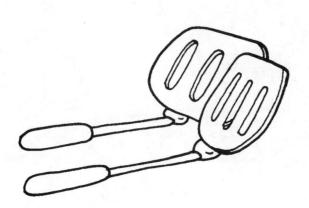

Story Tins

Large metal food tins or smaller coffee cans can make a fun surface for magnet storytelling. These surfaces can also be covered with self-stick paper. Cover several tins with a variety of backgrounds, and place the appropriate magnetic characters in the tins. Your children will love taking turns choosing a tin for storytime.

Magnet Sources

There are many kinds of magnets that you can buy for your magnetboards. Some of the best magnets to use for storytime activities are listed below.

+ Keep your eyes open for free magnets used for advertising purposes. These are usually flat magnet strips or sheets with advertising on the front. They are great for cutting up and attaching to the back of pictures or cut-out shapes. Tell parents you are collecting them and you'll soon have a large supply.

+ Small square and donut-shaped magnets made out of clay are great for teacher use because they are inexpensive and provide a strong magnetic hold. However, you must supervise young children very carefully with these because they break if dropped. These magnets are available in auto supply stores.

+ A favorite is the small, super-strong horseshoe-shaped magnet. Children love using these magnets to move story characters on which you have attached paperclips. (See the activity on page 45 for specific directions.)

+ Novelty magnets come in almost every shape and form. You may be able to find magnets in the shapes of people, foods, animals, household objects, and so on. Start a collection of these now, and you'll slowly build up enough to tell just about any children's story.

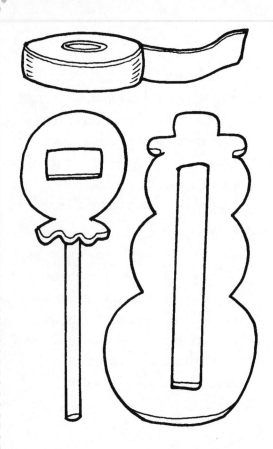

Magnetic Strip

Self-stick magnetic strip is available at craft stores. You can make almost anything into a magnetic character by sticking a small piece of magnetic strip to its back. Try some of the following ideas for making characters with magnetic strip.

+ Cut pictures of people, animals, and objects out of old magazines or greeting cards. Cover the figures with clear self-stick paper and attach magnetic strip to the backs of the pictures.

+ Take full-length pictures of your children. Cover the developed photos with clear self-stick paper and attach magnetic strip to the backs of the pictures.

+ From thin cardboard, cut out the shapes of the characters from one or two of your children's favorite stories. Cover them with clear self-stick paper and attach magnetic strip to the backs of the cutouts.

Photo Holders

Clear-plastic photo holders with magnets on the back are great for telling stories on a magnetboard. Magazine pictures, greeting-card cutouts, gift-wrap cutouts, and photos all fit easily in photo holders. The best part about using these is that they are easy to keep clean and they protect your cutouts. Set out several categories of pictures in holders (people, animals, objects, etc.) and let your children use them to tell and retell stories.

Magnetic Stands

Collect a variety of metal bookends. Use one of the techniques described on pages 43–44 to make a set of story characters for the story of the day. Gather the bookends and the characters. Place the characters on the bookends and move the bookends around to tell the story. Let your children use the characters and bookends to retell the story if they wish.

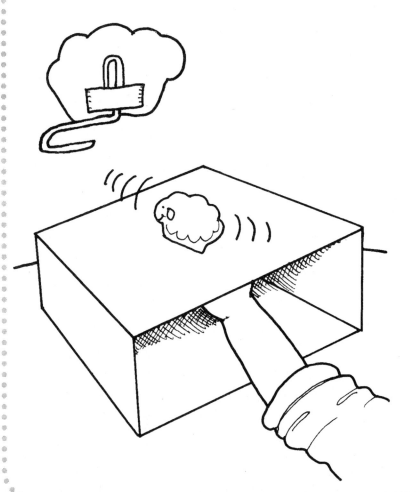

Movable Story Characters

This is a wonderful storytelling technique that children love. Cut out several story characters, making sure the bottoms of the characters are cut flat. Mount the pictures on heavy paper and cover them with clear self-stick paper. Then attach paper clips to the backs of the characters, as shown in the illustration. To use the characters, simply place them on a box top and run a strong magnet underneath the character. The magnet will attract the paper clip and move the character across the surface of the box.

Getting Kids Involved

Choosing the Topic

Children seem to enjoy stories more when they get to choose the subject matter. A good way to give your children choices is to select three books ahead of time. Tell your children the general topics of the books and let them select a story.

Following a Theme

After storytime, follow up by asking your children which part of the story they liked best. Encourage discussion of the topic by asking questions. For example, if your story was about rabbits, give information and ask questions about rabbits as they appeared in the story, as well as real rabbits. Then find a related story for the next day. Perhaps you could read a story about a farm, another rabbit story, or a story about carrots.

Books From Home

When children bring in books from home, place them in a special book bag instead of setting them out for everyone to share. A large cloth tote bag works well as a book bag, especially if you use fabric pens to decorate it with pictures of books. When storytime comes, draw one of the books out of the bag. The book bag approach will both protect the children's books and keep them separated from classroom books for easy retrieval when it's time to take them back home.

Choosing From a Book Basket

Select a variety of books and place them in a basket. Choose a child to come up and select the day's story. The story choice could be used as a reward or as a special treat for a birthday child, or you could simply implement the Book Basket choice method and let each of your children have a turn selecting a book.

Variation: Place three to six objects in a basket, each one representing a book you have available. Let a child choose an object and then select the book that the object represents.

Object Draw

It's easy to let children participate when you make up your own stories. One great way to get everyone involved is the Object Draw. To prepare, place enough small objects in a bag so that each child can draw one. Call your children together in a circle and begin a story. Pass the bag around, letting each child draw out one object. As soon as the object is visible, begin weaving it into your story. Children will especially love silly stories or stories that rhyme.

Deal-a-Story

Have your children sit in a circle. Deal one or two playing cards face down to each child. Select one child to turn over a card as you begin telling the story. Continue around the circle, letting each child turn over a card. Incorporate the numbers and pictures into the story as you go around the circle. Let the face cards represent people. For example, let the jack represent a boy or brother and the queen represent a woman or mother. Use the numbers to indicate how many animals, objects, or other things there are in the story. You might start with a story such as the following.

Ten bunnies went to town and found seven carrots at the home of the beautiful lady. The boy chased the rabbits into four holes. When the bunnies came out of the holes, there were two boys waiting to play ball. The bunnies played ball for six minutes, then five balloon salespeople appeared. The bunnies each bought three balloons (and so on).

Variation: Use any cards you have available. Concentration or lotto game cards, for example, would offer interesting pictures to weave into a story.

Photo Cube

Place pictures of objects familiar to the children in each side of a photo cube. Let your children take turns rolling the cube. When the cube lands, incorporate the objects in the pictures into your story. Children love this activity because they feel they are helping you create the story.

If you can't find a photo cube, simply attach pictures to all six sides of any small, cube-shaped box. Many stores sell gift boxes that are the perfect size, or you could use a dressing-table-size tissue box.

Felt Shapes

Put your flannelboard pieces to another use with this idea. Place flannelboard pieces representing people, animals, and objects into a bag. Give the bag to a child and let him or her draw a shape and hold it up. As each shape is drawn, weave it into your story.

Using Nursery Rhymes

Children love the repetition and silliness of nursery rhymes. For extra fun, let your children take turns filling in the rhyming word. Recite a familiar nursery rhyme such as "Mary Had a Little Lamb." When you get to the last line in the first stanza, "The lamb was sure to go," stop after the word "to" and point to a child. That child should say "go." Make sure each child in your group has a turn. Along with "Mary Had a Little Lamb," the rhymes listed below are particularly good for this activity.

Jack Be Nimble

Jack be nimble,

Jack be quick.

Jack jumped over

The candle _____.

Traditional

One, Two, Buckle My Shoe

One, two, buckle my _____.

Three, four, shut the _____.

Five, six, pick up _____.

Seven, eight, lay them _____.

Traditional

Row, Row, Row Your Boat

Row, row, row your boat

Gently down the stream.

Merrily, merrily, merrily, merrily,

Life is but a _____.

Traditional

Twinkle, Twinkle, Little Star

Twinkle, twinkle, little star

How I wonder what you _____.

Up above the world so high

Like a diamond in the _____.

Twinkle, twinkle, little star

How I wonder what you _____.

Traditional

Open-Ended Stories

Children love completing fill-in-the-blank stories because you can read the same story over and over and it will be different each time. You can have one child fill in all the blanks in a story, or you can invite more participation by letting a different child fill in each blank. Try one or more of the open-ended stories in this section.

Choosing a Pie

I went to the bakery

To buy a pie;

Which one to choose?

Oh me, oh my!

The biggest was a _____ pie.

The sweetest was a _____ pie.

The tallest was a _____ pie.

The juiciest was a _____ pie.

The smallest was a _____ pie.

Home from the bakery with my pie.

Can't wait till dinner,

And you know why!

Jean Warren

Waiter, Waiter

Waiter, waiter on the run,
I love _____.
Please bring me one.

Waiter, waiter dressed in blue,
I love _____.
Please bring me two.

Waiter, waiter by the tree,
I love _____.
Please bring me three.

Waiter, waiter by the door,
I love _____.
Please bring me four.

Waiter, waiter—sakes alive!
I love _____.
Please bring me five!

Jean Warren

Three Little Froggies

Three little froggies went down to the pond,

Down to the pond to play.

Along came a giant _____

And chased one froggie away!

Two little froggies went down to the pond,

Down to the pond to play.

Along came a giant _____

And chased one froggie away!

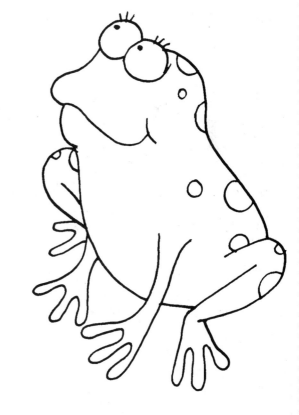

One little froggie went down to the pond,

Down to the pond to play.

Along came a giant _____

And chased that froggie away!

Now no little froggies went down to the pond,

Down to the pond to play.

Where do you think those froggies went

When they all hopped away?

Sue Foster

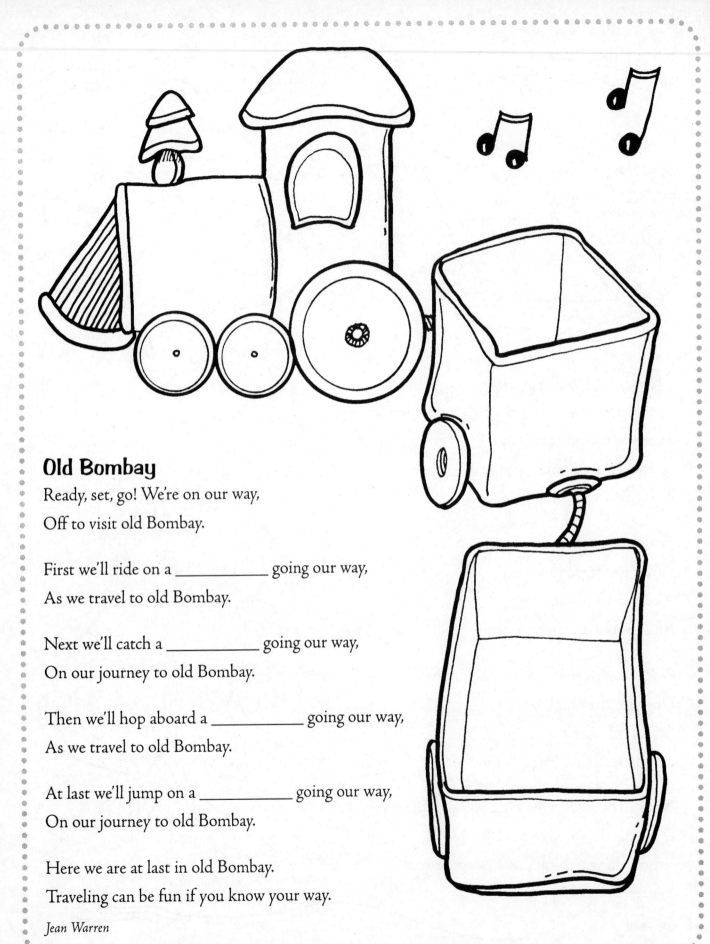

Old Bombay

Ready, set, go! We're on our way,
Off to visit old Bombay.

First we'll ride on a _____ going our way,
As we travel to old Bombay.

Next we'll catch a _____ going our way,
On our journey to old Bombay.

Then we'll hop aboard a _____ going our way,
As we travel to old Bombay.

At last we'll jump on a _____ going our way,
On our journey to old Bombay.

Here we are at last in old Bombay.
Traveling can be fun if you know your way.

Jean Warren

Vegetable Man

While I was walking down the street,

A Vegetable Man I happened to meet.

His head was a bumpy _____.

His arms were long _____.

His body was a large _____.

His legs were two green _____.

His feet were round _____.

His fingers and toes were _____.

He looked so good that on a hunch

I invited him to come home for lunch!

Jean Warren

Dictating Stories

Since dictation activities like this work best when done one-on-one, a great time to do them is when your children are engaged in other activities around the room. Encourage a child to tell you a story about what he or she is doing at the moment. The child may say something like "I am building a giant tower for the prince to live in. Bobby is helping me and we are going to put a flag up on the top." Be sure to write down exactly what the child says. Later, during storytime, read the stories and thank their authors.

Theme Stories

At storytime, discuss a general theme. Later ask your children to dictate short stories related to the theme. For example, if the theme is pumpkins, a child's story might go something like this: "My dad bought a pumpkin. We cut off the top and took out the seeds. We baked the seeds. They were good to eat." Later, read the stories at storytime along with a children's storybook about the theme discussed.

Extension: Make dictated stories part of your reading area by saving them in a three-ring binder. Have the children add a picture to their dictated stories, if desired. Let the children read through the binder whenever they wish. Read the dictated stories aloud at storytime several times a month. Add to the binder throughout the year.

Picture Stories

This activity bridges storytime with art time. When your children are painting pictures at the easel, take the time to have the children dictate stories about the pictures. Later, when the pictures are dry, call up each child during storytime. Let the child hold up the picture as you read his or her story.

Hint: Make sure the children are done with their paintings before dictating their stories. If they aren't finished, the dictated story may not go with the completed picture.

Magazine Stories

Mount some pictures from old magazines on colored construction paper. Leave plenty of room at the top or bottom of the page for dictation. Encourage a child to select a picture and then dictate a story to you about what is happening in the picture. Write the child's exact words on the construction paper, continuing on the back if necessary. During storytime, have each child hold up the picture as you read his or her story.

Hint: Select pictures that show some sort of action. Children sometimes find it easier to tell a story when an action picture prompts them.

Shape Props

Have your children place simple shapes and symbols (like those shown in the illustration) in a line on the flannelboard. Let a child assign a word to each shape. (Additional words can be used between the symbols to connect the story ideas.) Start with simple one-line stories, and then gradually encourage your children to "write" longer ones. The children can use the same shapes to make different stories depending on the words assigned to the shapes. For example, one child may place symbols on the flannelboard and read a story like this: "The mother bear and baby bear ran down to the lake. They caught three fish and took them home." Another child may interpret the same symbols like this: "The truck and the little car drove over the mountain and stopped at a big town. They stayed three days and then went home." What kind of stories can the children tell using the symbols below?

Scene Props

Kids really enjoy this story participation activity. Describe the characters in your story, or tell a story familiar to your children such as "The Three Billy Goats Gruff." Ask one of your children to look around the room to find something you could use for the large goat, the medium-size goat, and the small goat. Then have the children find something to use for a mountain, a bridge, and a troll. As long as things are in the right proportions, it does not matter what they choose. Tell the story, using the props chosen by your children. Sometimes it is a little silly, but it always makes for a fun, interesting storytime.

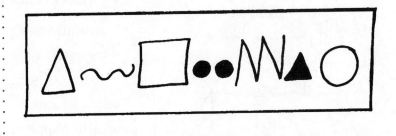

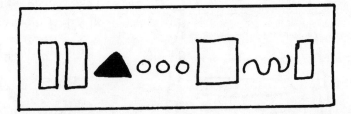

Dress-up Props

Set out a box of dress-up clothes and small props. Try to include many different types of clothing and props in the box, such as pants, dresses, uniforms, hats, coats, and baskets. Let three or four children come up and choose props to create a character. Then make up a story incorporating all of these characters and let the children act out their parts in the story.

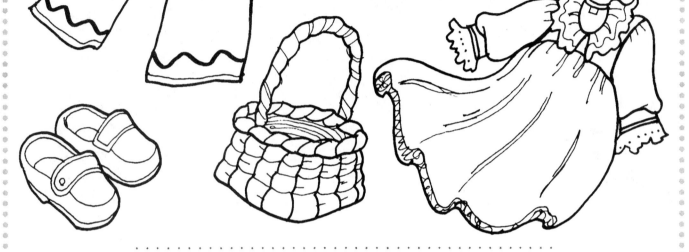

Masks

Let your group decorate simple paddle masks (paper plates attached to jumbo craft sticks) with yarn, markers, or feathers to create story characters. Then have them bring their paddle masks to storytime. Choose three or four children at a time to hold up their masks. Make up a story about these characters. Let each child stand and act out his or her part as you talk about it in the story.

Story Sounds

Most stories contain some sounds. Let your children participate by providing the sounds at the appropriate times. Ideas for generating common sounds include pouring water from one pitcher to another to simulate water running, and slapping thighs to represent running horses. Other sounds your children might like to make are animal sounds, lightning, musical sounds, pounding, and knocking. Stories like "Too Much Noise" are especially great for this type of participation.

Movement Stories

Stories often provide opportunities for children to participate in actions that keep them involved. These parts can be assigned to individuals as well as large groups. For example, if you are reading a story and you come to a place where horses gallop across a field, have your children gallop across the room and back. If sailors should row across a bay in a story, the children could pretend to row. Let your group begin marching in place if you are telling a story about a band or a parade.

Dramatizations

Help your children plan a mini-dramatization to perform as you reread a story. The dramatizations should be kept extremely simple. Since preschool children usually prefer to be part of a group where nothing hinges on a single individual, try not to single out one child if possible. If it's necessary, ask for volunteers and let children take turns. Props can be added but are not necessary. Children love it when you also take an active role in the dramatization. However, try to keep most of the decision making in the hands of your children.

Mini-Musicals

Let your children help you create simple songs that tell a story, sung to familiar tunes. Practice these songs with your children and have them tell the story in this musical way.

What Happens Next?

While reading a story, take advantage of the opportunities to stop and ask your children to guess what will probably happen next. Value all responses. This activity usually encourages children to listen more carefully and pay better attention because they will want to be able to guess where the story is heading.

What Is the Story About?

A good way to get your children interested in the plot of your story is to tell them the title and then let them guess what the story is about before you begin reading. Whether they guess right or wrong, their interest will be piqued and their attention will be greater when you begin the story.

Different Endings

After reading a story, take time to discuss the ending. Did your children like the ending? How might the ending have been different? Accept and discuss as many different endings as the children suggest.

Experimenting with different endings helps children develop their creative thinking skills. It is especially useful when children begin to write their own stories to know that there are multiple possibilities for the beginning, middle, and ending of stories.

Open-Ended Questions

Stimulate discussion by asking open-ended questions after you read a story. Ask questions such as these: "What do you think Corduroy was thinking when he saw Lisa and her mother shopping in the store?" "Where do you think Harry will go next time he leaves home?" Accept all answers.

Tell It Again!

After reading a story, retell the story, letting your children take turns telling what happened next. Only fill in the parts that they are unable to recall. The story can be retold more than once, if desired.

Retelling stories, especially when you stop and let the children fill in missing parts, helps children develop their memory skills. If you repeat the story often enough, children will usually end up telling you most of the story themselves. As children remember what happened first, second, and so on, they are well on their way to learning sequencing and ordering, which will help them develop essential reading and math skills.

Sequence Cards

Make sets of simple sequence cards for several of your children's favorite stories. You can make the cards by drawing simple figures on large index cards or copying actual pages from the book and then coloring them with felt tip markers. After reading or telling a story, let your children arrange sequence cards in the proper order and retell the story.

Variation: Set out a flannelboard and felt characters after reading a story. Let your children retell the story using the felt characters. They might also incorporate other felt characters and props to make up new stories.

Gameboards

Make simple gameboards built around the theme, plot, and characters of your favorite stories. Simple start-to-finish games, such as the example shown at right, are best for 3- to 5-year-olds. Your children can enjoy the story plot again and again as they play the board game. You can create your own gameboards by covering an old one with paper. Set out any game pieces or use large, different-colored beads, buttons, or even small painted rocks.

Puzzles

Look for simple puzzles based on your children's favorite stories. Add these to your tabletop toy area. After a child completes the puzzle, encourage him or her to retell the story. You may need to ask a few questions or make a few suggestions to jog the child's memory of the story.

Selecting Stories for Young Children

Story Characters

When selecting books for young children, choose stories with a limited number of characters. Since preschool children have short attention spans, stories with three to six characters are best. Children will quickly catch on to the characters and be less confused and more interested in the story.

Story Plots

Preschool children need very simple plots. One main event in the story or one main idea works best. Young children have a hard time following complex plots, and once you lose them, it is almost impossible to regain their attention. Any tried-and-true favorites are usually fine. With younger preschoolers, try nursery tales such as "The Three Pigs" or "Goldilocks and the Three Bears," or any beginning Dr. Seuss stories. Older preschoolers will enjoy more complex, yet still simple, popular children's stories.

Story Familiarity

Children seem to enjoy stories more when they have some connection with them. A connection with everything in the story is unnecessary, but at least something in the story should have a special meaning to your children. For example, if your story is about a farmer who grows a giant turnip, make sure your children understand what a turnip is before you begin reading. Let them examine a turnip, feel it, understand a little about how it grows and what people do with turnips. When children are familiar with objects in the story, it is easier for them to focus during storytime.

Rhyming Stories

Children are drawn to stories that rhyme. Rhyming stories help children develop important language and prereading skills such as listening, focusing, recognizing rhyming words, and anticipating the end of each stanza. Capitalize on all of these special "side effects" of rhyming stories by including many of them in your library and reading them at storytime.

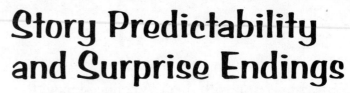

Story Predictability and Surprise Endings

Preschool children love predictable stories. They feel a certain amount of power when they know or can easily guess what is going to happen next. On the other hand, don't rule out surprise endings. If the rest of the story has been predictable, a small surprise at the end is something preschoolers love. They will enjoy it even more when you read it again because they'll know the surprise ending.

Repetitive Stories

Young children are drawn to repetitive stories because they lead to predictability and make stories easy to remember. Be sure to fill your bookshelf with stories that contain phrases and words that are repeated. Or try adding some predictability of your own. For example, say: "Trip, trap; trip, trap," each time one of the three billy goats crosses the troll's bridge, or repeat the huffing and puffing of the wolf at each of the three pigs' doors.

Stories filled with repetition also let young children feel like they are reading when they recite the phrases along with you as you are reading. This is especially great when a story is read one-on-one with a child.

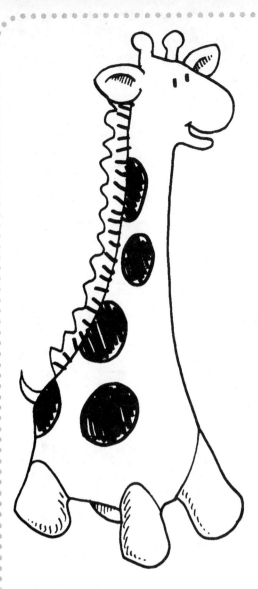

Story Length and Action

When selecting stories for preschoolers, remember that shorter is better, because young children lose interest in long stories. Story action is another important thing to keep in mind. Stories that lag will soon lose a young audience. The action should move at a predictable pace, not too fast, not too slow. Be aware that many children's books are written for the more advanced first- or second-grade listener and will fail to hold a younger audience, which is why short fables, folktales, and picture books are your best bets.

Illustrations

Clear, simple illustrations work best for preschoolers. Whether you are reading to a large group or a small group, the illustrations need to jump out at the children and help clarify the story. Stories illustrated with pictures that are small, busy, or hard to decipher from a distance should be reserved for one-on-one reading experiences when you can take the time to explain each picture.

Story Adaptability

When choosing a story, look for those you can adapt easily to use with flannelboard characters or simple puppets, or look for those that lend themselves to simple dramatizations. Whenever children have the opportunity to dramatize a short story, they will remember it, learn more from it, and have more fun with it.

Story Diversity

Diversity is an important element to remember when choosing stories. Look for a mix of environments—some inner-city, some suburban, and some rural settings. Also look for diversity in family situations, ages of the characters, and characters with disabilities. Because of the nature of preschoolers' need for security and their curious nature, they should be exposed to all types of locations and people in the stories they see and hear. A balance of content between familiar and unfamiliar elements is important to make them feel secure and to capture their curiosity about new situations.

Age-Appropriate Stories

For the most successful storytime experience, match the story to the age and comprehension level of your children. Be sure to check the vocabulary ahead of time. Are the words too hard for your children? Are they too easy? You know your children best. Pick books that meet the needs and vocabulary level of your children. Another thing to consider is whether your children will understand the concepts in the story. And, finally, are the paragraphs in the story too long or complex?

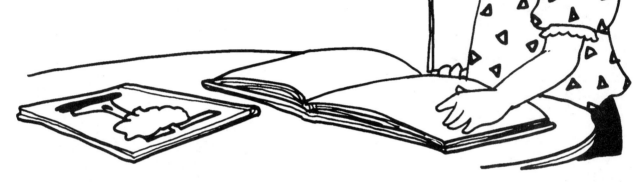

Favorite Stories

It is important that you choose stories that you personally like. Your love of the story will shine through your voice and expressions. Children will catch your enthusiasm and, hopefully, enjoy the story as much as you do.

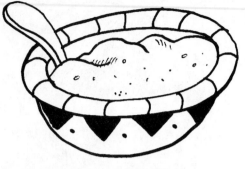

Adapting Stories

Parents and teachers sometimes find themselves in a situation in which they want to share with preschoolers a book that is written for older children. A good way to approach this problem is to first read the story yourself and then pretend to read the story to your children, replacing the original text with a much simpler version. Often, all you need to do is tell a story about the pictures in the book. Another method is to merely skip parts of the text that are long and complex.

Exploring Variations of Stories

A sure way to get a lively discussion from your children is to occasionally vary the elements of a familiar story and see if your children can detect the differences. For example, Goldilocks could walk into the house and find three bowls of ice cream. You could tell the story "The Country Rabbit and the City Rabbit." Or change the materials the three little pigs use to build their houses to newspapers, rope, and metal.

Adapting Characters to Fit Props

Often, you will want to read a favorite children's story and wish that you had a puppet to accompany the story. Why not make use of the puppets you have available and adapt the story to the puppet? For example, "Goldilocks and the Three Bears" can easily turn into "Raggedy Ann and the Three Bears," or "The Three Little Pigs" can become "The Three Little Dinosaurs."

Exploring Problems

Storytime is a wonderful time to explore problems your children may be having. You could adapt a story to be about a sick parent, a pet dying, or someone moving away. You could include a character who is in a wheelchair or has a hearing aid. You could also change characters to reflect family diversity. For example, introduce an interracial family or a family with divorced parents.

Personalizing Stories

Sometimes stories are more meaningful if you adapt them to fit your children. For example, you can adapt the story "Too Much Noise" by turning the house in the story into your room, and turning the noise into the quiet sound of children whispering and shuffling their feet. Your children will quickly identify with the children in the story and enjoy participating.

Adapting Folktales

Folktales are always evolving as new generations enjoy and adapt them to today's situations. You might try substituting women in some of the major roles. Below are some particularly good folktales you can adapt for your preschool children.

The Three Little Pigs—Make two of the pigs girls instead of boys.

The Three Billy Goats Gruff—Make the troll a woman.

Jack and the Beanstalk—Tell the story of Jill and the Beanstalk, or make the giant a woman.

The Three Sillies—Make the sillies women.

Goldilocks—Tell the story as if Goldilocks were a boy.

Creating Your Own Stories

Don't ever be afraid to make up your own stories. It is a great way to provide your children with meaningful stories adapted to meet their individual needs. By creating your own stories, you are also modeling to your children that all stories do not have to come from books.

Writing Your Own Rhyming Stories

Rhyming stories are especially fun to create yourself. A word of caution, though—if you are having trouble finding a rhyming word, don't use just any word that rhymes. Children know when something is contrived and does not make much sense. If you get stuck, try going back over your beginning lines. Changing these lines may help you discover a better, more fluid rhyme scheme.

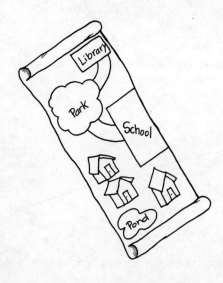

Story Stretching

Character Puppets

Stretching stories into other related activities during the day can really make literature come alive for your children. A great way to stretch storytime into art time is to make character puppets. If you read a story about a specific character or animal, give your children the materials necessary to make their own simple character puppets.

Story Placemats

Have your children draw simple pictures representing that day's story on a piece of construction paper. Turn their artwork into placemats by covering the construction paper with clear self-stick paper. When your children use their placemats during lunch or snacktime, they will have another opportunity to remember the day's story.

Variation: You can sometimes find rubber stamps of actual story characters, such as Winnie the Pooh or popular Disney stories. You can also find generic character and object stamps that will work for just about any story. Your children can use the stamps to decorate their placemats. Stickers also work well.

Class Mural

Stories often lend themselves to a class mural. Try to think of murals that allow your children to work on open-ended projects that you can put together to create a specific shape. For example if you have just read a story about love or hearts, make a large paper heart and cut it into as many pieces as you have children. Have the children decorate their pieces by spreading glue on them and sprinkling with red glitter. When the glue is dry, tape or pin all the pieces back together onto a bulletin board.

Variation: If you have just shared a seasonal story, let your children fingerpaint with pre-chosen colors. Cut their paintings into appropriate shapes for the colors, such as leaves, flowers, or trees. Attach the shapes to a bulletin board to make a class mural.

Easel Painting

If you give your children an opportunity to paint after hearing a story, chances are that their paintings will reflect some aspects of the story. You can promote this by setting out the appropriate colors of paint. This works especially well for seasonal stories. For example, set out red, pink, and white paint for Valentine's Day; green and red for Christmas; and green for St. Patrick's Day.

Environment Stories

Whenever a story takes place in a particular environment, you can follow up with hands-on experiences. Use your sand table to explore the desert and your water table to explore the ocean. Plant a garden outdoors or in a terrarium. Build mountains in the sandbox. Build a city in the block area. Help your children experience the environment of the book you have just read whenever possible.

Experiments

Many stories lead naturally into scientific explorations. After enjoying a classic story like "The Three Little Pigs," encourage your children to construct small houses. Have them determine which of the houses are the strongest by trying to blow them down. These experiments could lead to other explorations, such as deciding which building material would keep them warmest.

Animal Stories

Whenever your story is about a particular type of animal, take the opportunity to help your children discover things about the animal. For example, help your children find out what type of home the animal builds, what it eats, and what kind of climate it prefers.

Gardens

If your book happens to mention food, bugs, or flowers, you could consider exploring a garden. You might inspire your children to plant beans after hearing the story "Jack and the Beanstalk." A story about worms could lead to a worm-finding expedition. A story about flowers might lead to a field trip to a flower garden or perhaps planting marigolds.

Counting Characters

Many stories, such as "The Three Little Kittens," "Snow White and the Seven Dwarves," and "The Ten Little Bunnies," offer opportunities for counting. Choose children in your group to represent story characters and have them stand up or come to the center of the group. Then encourage everyone to help you count. Let the children return to their places as they are counted. Make sure everyone gets a chance to be counted.

Learning About Size

Size and proportions abound in children's stories. A wonderful story to use when exploring size concepts is "Goldilocks and the Three Bears." Provide your children with chances to set the table for the three bears and let them decide who gets each bowl, spoon, chair, and so on. There are many size-comparison activities you can develop from this story. Some other great stories to use for size comparisons are "The Big, Big Turnip," "The Three Billy Goats Gruff," "Pinocchio," and "The Princess and the Pea."

Measuring

Occasionally when a story contains a large object, let your children help you find out just how big the object probably was. Perhaps your story is about a whale. Look up the length of a whale with your children. Measure it out with a piece of yarn and then roll up the yarn. Let your children unroll the yarn to see just how long the whale really was.

Adding and Subtracting

Look for parts of stories where things are added or taken away, and dramatize these scenes with your children. Even if the story doesn't contain exact numbers, you can stretch a story with math dramatizations as a fun related activity afterward. For example, Little Red Riding Hood baked four cookies for her grandmother. Along the way she gave two of them to the wolf. How many did she have left?

Expanding Vocabulary

Stories provide rich opportunities for expanding your children's language. Encourage them to repeat favorite phrases and to act out small parts of a story. When talking with your children throughout the day, bring in words and sounds they experienced with the day's story.

Story Springboard

Instead of always looking for a completely different story to read each day, occasionally begin your story with a recap of a previous story. Then spring from a discussion of that story into an introduction of a new but similar story. Discuss similarities and differences of story characters and events with your children.

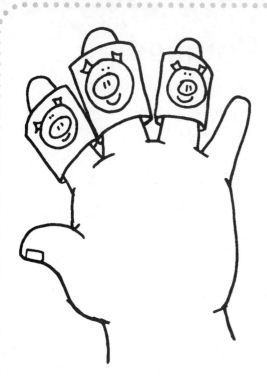

Puppet Plays

Together, make some of the simple finger puppets described on pages 27–28. Add features to turn the puppets into familiar story characters. Help each child make a Paper Plate Puppet Stage (page 32). Show your children how to use the puppets and the stages to dramatize their own versions of a favorite story.

Story Sharing

Hold a short sharing time after storytime, and let your children take turns retelling their favorite parts of the story. Accept all answers and encourage children to express themselves in complete sentences.

Rhymes

Storytime is a natural time to combine story enthusiasm with the learning of some new, short rhymes. If your story is about a cat, start or finish your story with some cat rhymes. Or, better yet, have your children help you make up rhymes that tell a bit of the story.

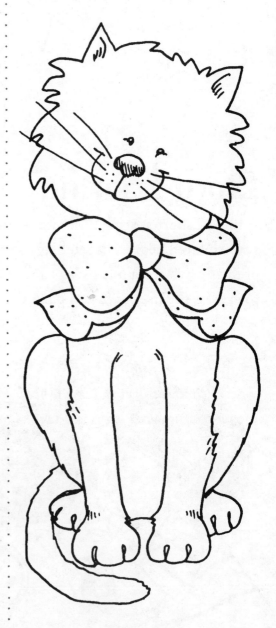

Dramatizations

Let your children choose a story and take turns acting out the parts. For example, they would probably love taking turns playing the family members in "The Big, Big Turnip." Dramatizing stories is a wonderful creative opportunity for your children—one that they will love to do often.

Music

Sing related songs or encourage your children to come up with the names of songs they feel would go with the day's story. You can also make up Piggyback® Songs with your children by singing new words to familiar tunes. Children love to feel that they helped write a song.

Movement

Look for stories that include weather conditions that children can dramatize. Children love to move like the wind, twirl like fall leaves, fall softly like the snow, drop like rain, or whirl like tornadoes. They also love to act out the movements of animals in stories. Have your children slink slyly like a cat, hop quickly like a bunny, or soar silently like an eagle.

Guest Speakers

When you have an opportunity to bring in a guest with a special skill, find a book that relates to that skill. For example, if your guest weaves and will bring in examples of woven goods, plan a story that involves weaving clothes or blankets, such as "The Emperor's New Clothes."

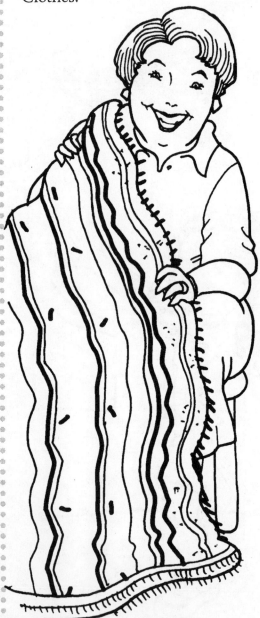

Field Trips

After a field trip to a special place, such as a fire station, a park, or a library, read related stories to your children. Let them make up stories about their experiences that you can add to your three-ring story binder (page 58). Your children will love dramatizing these stories after they visit the setting.

Maps

Preschool children do not really understand references to world maps, but when stories involve a neighborhood adventure, you can draw a simple neighborhood on butcher paper and indicate story places on your map. Later, your children can use cars and pretend figures with your map.

Board Games

Some popular children's books are now packaged with board games. This is a wonderful new concept that you can use to review many social situations as your children play the corresponding game. Playing board games provides a setting in which children need to interact with others to play. Before your children begin their game, quickly review manners such as taking turns, keeping our hands to ourselves, and talking in a quiet voice.

Modeling

When characters in a story model good behavior, take time to let your children act out the scene. Listening to a story about good behavior will have a positive influence on children, but modeling will reinforce the desired behavior even more.

Social Play

Preschool is a great time to begin teaching basic manners. Take advantage of pointing out the correct social behavior that appears in stories, such as saying "Please" and "Thank you," saying "Excuse me," telephone phrases, and greeting people.

Snacks

Look for stories that give you opportunities to bring in related snacks for your children. If the story was about cookies, for example, bring in several different types of cookies for your children to taste. If your story takes place in Mexico, bring in your favorite Mexican snack to share. Snacks are often bridges to understanding people from different cultures.

Recipes

If a story talks about biscuits, pies, or cakes, bring in your favorite simple recipe and let your children help make it. To turn this into a pre-reading activity, draw a rebus version of the recipe on large chart paper and let your children follow along as you make the recipe.

Totline® PUBLICATIONS

Teacher Resources

ART SERIES
Ideas for successful art experiences.
Cooperative Art
Special Day Art
Outdoor Art

BEST OF TOTLINE® SERIES
Totline's best ideas.
Best of Totline Newsletter
Best of Totline Bear Hugs
Best of Totline Parent Flyers

BUSY BEES SERIES
Seasonal ideas for twos and threes.
Fall • Winter • Spring • Summer

CELEBRATIONS SERIES
Early learning through celebrations.
Small World Celebrations
Special Day Celebrations
Great Big Holiday Celebrations
Celebrating Likes and Differences

CIRCLE TIME SERIES
Put the spotlight on circle time!
Introducing Concepts at Circle Time
Music and Dramatics at Circle Time
Storytime Ideas for Circle Time

EMPOWERING KIDS SERIES
Positive solutions to behavior issues.
Can-Do Kids
Problem-Solving Kids

EXPLORING SERIES
Versatile, hands-on learning.
Exploring Sand • Exploring Water

FOUR SEASONS
Active learning through the year.
Art • Math • Movement • Science

JUST RIGHT PATTERNS
8-page, reproducible pattern folders.
Valentine's Day • St. Patrick's Day •
Easter • Halloween • Thanksgiving •
Hanukkah • Christmas • Kwanzaa •
Spring • Summer • Autumn •
Winter • Air Transportation • Land
Transportation • Service Vehicles
• Water Transportation • Train
• Desert Life • Farm Life • Forest
Life • Ocean Life • Wetland Life
• Zoo Life • Prehistoric Life

KINDERSTATION SERIES
Learning centers for kindergarten.
Calculation Station
Communication Station
Creation Station
Investigation Station

1•2•3 SERIES
Open-ended learning.
Art • Blocks • Games • Colors •
Puppets • Reading & Writing •
Math • Science • Shapes

1001 SERIES
Super reference books.
1001 Teaching Props
1001 Teaching Tips
1001 Rhymes & Fingerplays

PIGGYBACK® SONG BOOKS
New lyrics sung to favorite tunes!
Piggyback Songs
More Piggyback Songs
Piggyback Songs for Infants
and Toddlers
Holiday Piggyback Songs
Animal Piggyback Songs
Piggyback Songs for School
Piggyback Songs to Sign
Spanish Piggyback Songs
More Piggyback Songs for School

PROJECT BOOK SERIES
*Reproducible, cross-curricular project
books and project ideas.*
Start With Art
Start With Science

REPRODUCIBLE RHYMES
*Make-and-take-home books for
emergent readers.*
Alphabet Rhymes • Object Rhymes

SNACKS SERIES
Nutrition combines with learning.
Super Snacks • Healthy Snacks •
Teaching Snacks • Multicultural Snacks

TERRIFIC TIPS
Handy resources with valuable ideas.
Terrific Tips for Directors
Terrific Tips for Toddler Teachers
Terrific Tips for Preschool Teachers

THEME-A-SAURUS® SERIES
Classroom-tested, instant themes.
Theme-A-Saurus
Theme-A-Saurus II
Toddler Theme-A-Saurus
Alphabet Theme-A-Saurus
Nursery Rhyme Theme-A-Saurus
Storytime Theme-A-Saurus
Multisensory Theme-A-Saurus
Transportation Theme-A-Saurus
Field Trip Theme-A-Saurus

TODDLER RESOURCES
Great for working with 18 mos–3 yrs.
Playtime Props for Toddlers
Toddler Art

Parent Resources

A YEAR OF FUN SERIES
Age-specific books for parenting.
Just for Babies • Just for Ones •
Just for Twos • Just for Threes •
Just for Fours • Just for Fives

LEARN WITH PIGGYBACK® SONGS
*Captivating music with
age-appropriate themes.*
Songs & Games for…
Babies • Toddlers • Threes • Fours
Sing a Song of…
Letters • Animals • Colors • Holidays
• Me • Nature • Numbers

LEARN WITH STICKERS
*Beginning workbook and first reader
with 100-plus stickers.*
Balloons • Birds • Bows • Bugs •
Butterflies • Buttons • Eggs • Flags •
Flowers • Hearts • Leaves • Mittens

MY FIRST COLORING BOOK
*White illustrations on black back-
grounds—perfect for toddlers!*
All About Colors
All About Numbers
Under the Sea
Over and Under
Party Animals
Tops and Bottoms

PLAY AND LEARN
Activities for learning through play.
Blocks • Instruments • Kitchen
Gadgets • Paper • Puppets • Puzzles

RAINY DAY FUN
*This activity book for parent-child fun
keeps minds active on rainy days!*

RHYME & REASON STICKER WORKBOOKS
*Sticker fun to boost
language development and
thinking skills.*
Up in Space
All About Weather
At the Zoo
On the Farm
Things That Go
Under the Sea

SEEDS FOR SUCCESS
*Ideas to help children develop
essential life skills for future success.*
Growing Creative Kids
Growing Happy Kids
Growing Responsible Kids
Growing Thinking Kids

THEME CALENDARS
Activities for every day.
Toddler Theme Calendar
Preschool Theme Calendar
Kindergarten Theme Calendar

TIME TO LEARN
Ideas for hands-on learning.
Colors • Letters • Measuring •
Numbers • Science • Shapes •
Matching and Sorting • New Words
• Cutting and Pasting •
Drawing and Writing • Listening •
Taking Care of Myself

Posters
Celebrating Childhood Posters
Reminder Posters

Puppet Pals
Instant puppets!
Children's Favorites • The Three Bears
• Nursery Rhymes • Old MacDonald
• More Nursery Rhymes • Three
Little Pigs • Three Billy Goats Gruff •
Little Red Riding Hood

Manipulatives
CIRCLE PUZZLES
African Adventure Puzzle

LITTLE BUILDER STACKING CARDS
Castle • The Three Little Pigs

Tot-Mobiles
*Each set includes four punch-out,
easy-to-assemble mobiles.*
Animals & Toys
Beginning Concepts
Four Seasons

Start right, start bright!